THE TOWN

PRIYAM GANGULI

First Published in May 2023

ISBN: 978-93-5704-035-8

BLUEROSE PUBLISHERS

www.BlueRoseONE.com
info@bluerosepublishers.com
+91 8882 898 898

Cover Design:
Muskan Sachdeva

Typographic Design:
Pooja Sharma

Distributed by: BlueRose, Amazon, Flipkart

Author Introduction

Priyam Ganguli is currently an undergraduate student of Engineering at Thapar Institute of Engineering & Technology. An avid guitarist, Priyam has a penchant for the mysteries of the universe, and ever since he was a kid, he has pondered the mysteries of the universe its existence, and the changes. These have captivated him to think of incidents and their connection to our daily lives. Priyam feels that just as the next change in this universe is beyond one's control, so is the forthcoming incident in one's life! In this book, he writes about what changes one's view of life when we come to know just how much we don't know in this vast world. This book has been written in such a way that the readers can live the same way the main protagonist has. The author is a very curious person and is always wondering what will happen next and his work will make you ask too what will happen next.

The Town

Welcome to the world of Ryan Anderson. Located in India lies a place away from civilization, small town nestled deep in a forest, on the mountains, world of wonders. The world of Tejangolan. Far from the bustling cities and crowded streets. People living in tranquillity amidst the quiet beauty of nature

The Britishers founded Tejangolan, but its history is much older than that.

Secrets waiting to be revealed, from ancient caverns to treacherous forests.

Tejangolan is a place with mysteries-mysteries lost to the time.

Do you dare to enter the world of Tejangolan reader?

Contents

Epilogue-1

Arrival

Chapter-1

It Begins

It was him from the start. He knew everything. He was always one step ahead of me at every turn.

I am no match for him, but I must try before letting go. This may be the last entry I make. I don't know who will win, but I will not lose anyone anymore.

(As the sky turns black, everything fades away)

Year-2022

On 31st October, my family, the Andersons, consisted of me, my parents, my 11-year-old sister. We moved to a remote town called Tejangolan.

As you may know, almost no one celebrates Halloween in India, but this place does; why?

May be because this town was known to be founded by a foreigner established as one of the Indo-British towns, it wanted to keep its traditions alive.

The construction of the houses and shops of this town were exciting and peculiar. I wonder the place appeared as if they could survive the Apocalypse. I don't know why I felt like I have been here before.

I couldn't share my feelings with my parents; It might sound irrational and farther from the truth. My bonding with my sister was firm. She was the only one to be an ardent believer of my figments of imagination and feelings. She was desperately awaiting to go on an extended camping trip next week. I will miss her.

Though we all were tired from traveling for the last twelve hours, we decided not to unpack much today and rest. It was supposed to be the well-furnished house but further from reality.

Strangely, the extra spurt of energy and zeal to get my room arranged overnight was quite contradictory to my usual behaviour of finding good reasons to evade from hard work. I teamed up with my sister to arrange our rooms tonight. We were busy putting in our rooms when the doorbell rang and lights went off just then due to power cut. Being brother sister, we often get same thought transference. "Who would have come at this hour." We both ended up saying it almost same time. It must have been the kids celebrating Halloween out for trick or treat. I had read about this tradition but never thought of ever experiencing it. I opened the door. Astonished to see a tall figure in a long black cloak, hat, and mask on his face. I could hear him saying quite loud the following.

"Beware !!! The three keys you must seek. The hands will increase, so will the lock; hurry before the dead walk, and the world perishes."

Now, this was beyond my comprehension. Nevertheless I invited him in and tried to look for candle. I found a strange looking one lying in an corner shelf. It had a peculiar glow unlike others. As soon as I took it to the visitor it blew out on its own and there was thick smoke around.

By the time smoke was cleared the man just disappeared in the dark, I was left aghast with doubt. Had I imagined the whole thing? Was the man even real? Or was he just a figment of my imagination, a product of my overactive imagination?

But the reality got evident as soon as I saw a note lying on the door mat. It was getting something mysterious; I told my sister but couldn't tell about the cryptic message written on the note. She made me feel light by calling it a prank, It appeared normal to her on a Halloween night but I was just not able to shake it off. I tried hard to read and understand the message. I got perplexed with when my eyes fell on the text written in the last

"Beware!!! fate awaits." You."

Chapter-2

The Three Journals

After a brain racking exercise for three days which made me so restless. At last, I cracked the cryptic message written in a mirror inverse code. It was a description of a place right next to my house only.

I reached out to the back yard of the abandoned mansion next to me to the same old tree as described in the message. I discovered three journals wrapped in vellum or parchment like material placed inside the tree hollow. These books seemed like journals. I brought them home hurriedly.

I named the first journal as 'The CODEX' since It's text was written in an unknown cryptic language.

The second one was named as THE "DEVIL'S HEART." This journal referred to many mysteries of this strange town of Tejangolan, about creatures beyond my wildest thoughts.

The third book was blank, but its pages were thick, white and had a strange texture. The best title of this journal I could think of was to name it as "THE WHITE VOID"

I was pretty sure about the connection with saying of the man with these journals. I was in a state of ecstatic consciousness with my new discovery. These journals were the three keys that would unlock the mystery?? I had to also unravel about 'hands' the mysterious man referred to?

My parents moved from Punjab in north of India to this remote town called Tejangolan. Nestled in the Himalayan mountains in India. It seemed the remote outlying town surrounded with dense forest around, was yet to be explored. Not much information about the town was registered in the records. It was pretty apparent that very few people tread on such a remote place. My parents are scientists and were invited to conduct some extra ordinary research.

Landing in such fascinating places, though, was a sheer coincidence but enough to continue to fire imaginations of any adventurer and explorer like me. As we got close to the town, the stunning architecture was captivating. There was something truly magical about this town.

Chapter-3

The House Of Nothing

5.00 pm

I joined the middle school located in the outskirts of the town. The school was connected to the town with a long road with forest on its right side stretched around 10 km. As expected, school was quite a dull and monotonous place. Attending classes and homework sessions were as boring as it could be.

The good thing was that I made friends with whom I could hang out with. They were my classmates and we were neighbours as well. We all went by the same bus. The bus stop happened to be our common meeting place. That's precisely where I met Michael, Tannie and Julia for the first time. We felt an unexpected jolt of connection between ourselves, as if we've known each other forever and were meant to meet. There was automatically a spark of solid sense of connection. I felt the fire had been laid for a firefly friendship to ignite. Soon we had a sense of rapport and connection were "on the same wavelength", to converse and share. Despite monotony we would find ways to make our life interesting.

I discovered the abandoned mansion having big old tree hollow in its courtyard where I found the journals was to be called as "**the House of nothing**". It was located at the entrance of the town. The architecture was so strange that one could not see anything from a distance. At just 20m distance, no one can make out as if any building even exists. It seemed to be an old abandoned mansion. It was right next to my house. My house and this one was seemed to be the oldest of all the houses in the vicinity. Besides these two buildings, all other houses were little distant from each other.

Since I brought the three journals home, I have been experiencing poltergeist activity nearly daily. Sometimes, I could see moving shadows as if someone were dwelling there.

I knew in the old houses, the wood tends to settle and turn home to be a draftee, but there have been times I heard the creaking sound of wood and seen moving shadows as if someone had just walked through the rooms in the adjacent house. Has this ever happened to whoever lived before we moved into the house? It would be fascinating to check the history of the

‘House of nothing’ through the local town clerk for the names of previous owners.

Four of us, being angst teenagers, were keen to investigate more on this ‘House of nothing.’

The only thing people knew was that the house I was dwelling in now, once belonged to a guy named Bhaskara. Who lived alone. Bhaskara was known by locals as a very private, reserved and mysterious character and he rarely interacted with anyone and kept to himself most of the time. He remained an enigma and people in town were wary of him and chose to keep a distance. It was told to me that one day he just disappeared. Nobody knew about his whereabouts.

Who was this Bhaskara, and what secrets did he have? There was something about the person that might help to solve all of the mystery, or he could be just an average guy who lived here before me. Will I ever meet him?

Chapter-4

Secrets

The town Tejangolan hiding deadly secrets, something sinister, there was something very unexplainable going on. I observed some students in the school with uncanny tattoos as if they were part of some secret society or a cult. My friend Michael told me, people believe they were group of students who were tired of being bullied and ostracized by their peers. They formed secret society to gain sense of belonging and power.

10.00 pm at the house.

I opened the second journal. What I read next sounded like a myth. Could it be true, or could it be just a made-up story.?

This journal, "**the devil's heart,**" had a mind of its own. The moment I opened the book, it automatically flipped to a page that had a strange sketch and details about some creature called.

The Haenbachu

Power- expert at fire [source-fear]

Weakness- unknown [found at Clintons house yard]

There was nothing else mentioned. and as soon as I was done reading, the journal closed on its own!

These creatures are not to be taken lightly as they may hunt or kill people by instinct.

The next day 6:00pm

This bizarre situation regarding the mysteries and strange stuff happening around was making me feel claustrophobic and I was desperately in need to be resurrected.

The one thing that was still haunting my mind was whether I can trust my friends , because of the three half notes I found at the end of the journals, stated, **"Trust no one."** I have to be very careful and decide who all can I trust in this strange town of secrets

Chapter-5

Mysteries, A Universe Full Of Them.

8 am at house, Sunday

It was a bright sunny day. I thought of grabbing the day to jot down the following checklist from my mind's mystery box based on the series of recent observations and incidents

- The mystery man who appeared in the evening of Halloween.
- The delivered message
- The strange candle with peculiar flame that blew off on its own
- The mystery behind the journals
- The mystery of the creature Haenbachu

- The mystery behind experiencing the sense presence effect. When I felt I am being watched and followed, someone actually tailing me, I could hear footsteps, I had the sense as if I am not alone in the room
- The glitches on my clock every day at exactly 4:50 am and 9:15 pm.
- Knowing Bhaskara was also on my checklist.

I now desperately needed a team to unravel this series of mystery. I would need a base to execute the operations. A definite plan and schedule to keep track of everything happening. A way to sneak in and out of the ground to my house, Tools or weapons to defend.

At that point in time the best feasible conclusion were the 'House of nothing' would be a perfect choice for the base. About the team, I decided to go by my gut feeling of firefly spark of friendship and not to test them. Julia Moore, Michael Day, Tannie Hill, and myself Ryan Anderson for this entrusted reconnaissance mission.

I was thrilled to learn that this town had given me a purpose and filled my life with adventure.

(Unaware of the future, Ryan Anderson dreams of a perfect adventure, but he did not know what awaits him is far more perilous. Ordinary will not do. Only the ones with the courage of a lion and a heart of steel survive here.

He must be ready for what comes because if he was not, the world as he knew it would never be the same.)

Chapter-6

Uniting The Mystery Hunting Team

The first mystery- the legend of Haenbachu

Saturday morning,

At school, I told my friends that I am very curious to explore the town's nightlife. They all quickly agreed to my wish as if I had planned an adventure trip.

As it got darker, all of us met at my place We had the dinner together, afterwards and we went out to explore the town. I was feeling terrible for not revealing them why I wanted to explore the town. I carried salt pellets in a pouch to combat paranormal creatures.

It was nearly midnight when clock stuck twelve o'clock, We were walking on the same stretch of road that was on our way to school having forest on our right.

The streets were empty, with street lights flickering and cold wind gushing. I was walking quite close to the woods and keeping a track at the locations where the *Haenbachu* could be' according to the second journal.

All of sudden a tall man with black hair and scaly skin was right there in front of us at a distance. Though there was nothing paranormal but I was quite sure of that we were going to have an encounter with the creature Haenbachu that I read in the journal. But never expected to have it coming so soon. I joined the conversation with the friends, they were referring to seeing the man at the distance in the midnight was strange. I too almost believed that it was some stranger only but my mind was giving me some sinister signals of Haenbachu being around.

I told my friends to let us all go back home.

Chapter-7

Not What He Seemed

1 am, midnight

We were returning home when I stopped and looked back; and stood frozen for a while as what I saw just chilled me to the core. Behind me stood a burnt creature whom we saw at the distance and my friends had just treaded a distant apart as they might not have realized I am lagging behind. I was terrified but I knew that I had to face my fears. I decided to confront the creature head on It was like anything I had ever seen before

His eyes were glowing as light, and he had a tilted head and a vast cape, one arm was broken, and I could see the bony arms while his mouth was open and drooling with strange greenish saliva. Suddenly he changed his appearance into 'Haenbachu' exactly like the one I saw in the Devil's Heart. I was too petrified to move, but something inside me reacted, and I pushed the Haenbachu away, Julia turned back, but we were at a distance where they couldn't see the creature. In the moment of sheer panic, I threw salt pellets that I kept it for good luck. The Haenbachu started dwindling and vanished. This all happened just in the fig of moment before my friends could turn back and look for me. I quickly ran up to my friends and was too much caught up with fear.

Sunday

I finally came back to my senses when I got up after a long sleep. Thinking how I got saved. Was it my throwing salt pellets that helped or someone whom I sense its presence came to my rescue remained a mystery. The journals must be referred to know if there was any perfect way to overpower such creatures in this town.

I noticed another note lying on my table. I remembered vaguely to have crossed the same masked man while I was entering my house after the incident. This note was definitely from him again. The message said the following

"The creatures born of this world and old are forever trapped in the curse never foretold".

My life kept on getting weirder and weirder. First, I fought a creature as giant as a man with salt pellets! Then this masked man in black kept surprising me with all these prophecies and notes.

This town is an endless puzzle. The more I try to solve It . the more complicated it was getting.

6:00 pm

I reencountered the masked man early morning, He bumped into me, instead of a note, It was a bag of mist balls. I heard him loud and clear to be careful and watch over the tree hollow across my house where I had discovered found the journals.

Before I could ask what, he was talking about, he disappeared by walking away into the fog.

Chapter-8

Behind You

The mist balls which were like tiny capsules filled with strange stuff. The reference of the same were given in the "devils' heart". A mandusk sap which not only wards off wild beasts but heals body rather instantly like a miracle.

Michael and me were once again heading towards the woods. There was a strange attraction which was difficult to resist. I took the second journal 'the Devil's heart' along with me of course the bag of mist balls given by the masked man.

A few minutes later

As soon as we entered the dark forest, I noticed a sudden change in Michael. He started sweating in the cold, his pupils were dilated, and I could almost hear his heartbeat as It was beating that loudly. He insisted on returning, explaining that it was not a good time since it will be dark soon.

Did he have premonition something untoward going to happen. 'Devil's Heart flipped open to a page having a description of some creature with a ghastly mutant hound-like beast and a comical name. The shadow wolf tiger,' The creature looked like this.

[Weakness: not known

Power: optical manipulation

Strength: dark air Elementa

Beware: since only its face has been seen, its hunt is challenging.]

I felt something following me, and my gut was all twisted in knots about turning back to look. The fear, the confusion, the adrenaline rushed in as there laid the shadow wolf tiger looking at me with its yellow eyes and ghastly appearance

I was holding Michael hands tightly to run as we weren't expecting this but he froze there, and I ended up leaving my poor friend alone.

I barely escaped, but could not help Michael. He was trapped. I was feeling miserable that Michael was left behind to be preyed.

All I knew about the "shadow wolf tiger" that it had powers that could mess with the mind of its prey, and to the extent that could control its mark, Michael was not safe. He was hypnotized. The "devil's heart" did mention a cure that brings back cognition to the prey. I took out the mist balls made up of mandusk. That had healing properties.

After wandering in the dark forest for hours, I finally found Michael, but he could barely move. Trapped in some strange web the shadow wolf tiger made, I quickly got Michael out of the web and then cured him with the sap.

It was a howl, a chilling cry that echoed through the trees.

The tall menacing creature lurking in the shadow with glowing eyes and razor sharp claws saw me and attacked with its tenacious fang, and as soon as it struck, I did not hesitate and threw the mist balls at it blocking its view. I ran towards it and quickly poured mandusk sap over it as it howled.

It just faded away like the Haenbachu.

It was great that Michael couldn't recall anything otherwise it would have taken a toll on his mind. This had given me a space too to decide that how would I tell Michael about this incident how Michael when was paralyzed and trapped in the web

I was wondering if there were some way of knowing beforehand, the dangers the town was likely to face.

Chapter-9

Unexpected Doors And Windows

The door to the future was more than one, but only one window led to the past. The window was proof of the past, whereas the doors were either the entrance to the end, or proof of possibilities.

I discovered The "devil's heart "opened up new page for me, which meant, I had to be ready to face creature called,

Picheals.

[Power- quick and annoyance

Source- of origin yet to be determined.

To stop it, use cages made from wood.]

It was once again now the time to be together with friends in the town to scuff out the mysteries lurking in the shadows.

Next night at 10:00 pm

Amidst of my intrusive thoughts about revealing the secrets of the journals and the creatures lurking in every nook and cranny of the town to my friends,

While walking towards the right side, we heard a shattering sound. It came from a window of one of the shops. Michael gasped as he sees an unruly creature staring at him from the window of a shop. He was too petrified so were Tannie and Julia

I went closer and knew that it's an encounter with **Picheals.** I was all prepared. I knew now a way to convert into a tiny creature and trap it by magical spell. I carried it in my bag.

The glitches of the time piece at 4.50am woke me up felt as if someone sitting on my couch. I gasped and turned around as I heard his loud and clear voice saying

"This is not over; you are being

watched, do not give up."

It was none other than the masked man. whose identity had been an enduring mystery. His eyes were fixed on me. I garnered courage to ask him

how did you get in here?

While still trying to process my shock

"I have my ways"

The masked man replied.

He came to warn me again that I was in danger. Without wasting even a moment I asked the reason for wearing a mask and why he kept his identity remained veiled. The next moment he removed the mask. He told me that his name was Arman Plangad and if his identity got revealed to anyone, he would immediately be ripped off." He had an intense look on his face with determined eyes. I listened to his story with a mix of fear and scepticism It all seemed too far -fetched to be true, but there was something about his intensity that made me believe it.

I realised his mystery endured because the unknown truth of his identity tantalized I was drawn towards it. Not knowing who he was left me open to speculation. Arman Plangad was a real - and frightening human being. At the same time, he will remain anonymous, forever an elusive shadow just beyond our reach.

Before he could disappear, he got me two more journals

Chapter-10

More Journals?

24 December 2022

I finally had the five journals. I named the book of alchemy, "Alchemy grimoire," and the locked book was called "sealed knowledge."

As I was walking toward my house. I saw a horrifying creature floating in the air. I did not know what it was, but it scared me to death, and all it took was a whisper. You could feel the hatred coming from it.

As that creature floated, it moved strangely. It lay within a dense fog, watching me with its big eyes around, which pushed those tentacles.

I am sure it could feel my fear as it came closer to me right in front of my face and whispered in an eerie tone ", stay away from the truth.".

I was paralyzed with fear as I stood there in the middle of the trend when I blinked; it was gone. The most horrifying thing ever is the being with myriad eyes!

End Of Epilogue-1

Epilogue-2:
Enter the Darkness

Chapter-11

Growing Consternations

25th December 2022

Colorful lights hung outside every house, and a giant tree stood in the middle of the town. They were decorated from top to bottom with streamers, ornaments, and a massive star.

It was Christmas. As the Christmas tree flickered and shone a bright light, the giggles and chuckles of children echoing throughout the town. It almost seems fictitious. The exhilaration, it 'seems, masks the true nature of this town.

Tejangolan was more than just a town. It was a ruse, and those who fell for it never could see it coming.

What happened when fear was the only emotion you felt? You were trapped in utter confusion, and there was no way out.

The monstrosity I saw, the very thing that trapped me in constant panic, was much more than what I witnessed. The devil's heart called it '***Neilalive.***"

A being with immeasurable power and malevolent nature. Neilalive used negativity from the dark void. Only a little was known about the dark hole.

The "devil's heart" clearly instructs not to trust Neilalive ever!

The creature's appearance was shown differently in the devil's heart than I saw. The question remains, why now, out of all the time, did Neilalive chose to choose to reveal itself?

Later that night,

I walked past my house to the Dark Forest and saw it staring right at me. As it surged toward me, a shining sword appeared in my hand.

I stabbed the monstrosity with it, but it wasn't over when I pulled out the blade. The monstrosity pushed me with its remaining strength downwards; I felt like I was constantly falling, and the shock woke me up.

When I woke up from this dream, I looked at the mirror near my bedside and heard a whisper, "I have answers to your questions, Ryan Anderson." Too exhausted, I went back to sleep, thinking it was part of the dream.

I often asked myself, “What makes this town different?” could there be an incident which made Tejangolan this way?

Year-1829

"Foundation Era"

As the birds flew across grey skies filled with dust and ashes, Bhaskar and Raj walked across the woods, on a remote land later named Tejangolan. Both known to be strategic and visionary mystery explorers. With peril and exacerbated by the current urgency to build back better toolkit. They set out to the dense forest of Tejangolan in search of an ancient artifact that was used to send telepathic messages. Particularly amongst the perilous sinister creatures.

The intriguing conversation between them were related to extracting energies from their experiments on otherworldly creatures.

"Has it begun, Bhaskar?" said Raj. "Not yet, my friend, some more time is needed" replied Bhaskar. The process was almost complete. It should be working soon; we would be the first to witness

Suddenly, he noticed through peripheral vision a flash of a creature from the dark forest. Bhaskar tried to punch its face but there was no effect he was slammed on the ground. Bhaskar knew the consequences if the creature overpowered. It will be a disaster.

What happened next just knocked the wind out of Bhaskar. The creature leapt and latched on top of Raj, grabbed him and drag him long towards a ravine. Bhaskar screamed. Raj was screaming too. Raj screamed ", Bhaskar, you promised me!"

Year-2022

location: Tejangolan, deep in the dark forests.

(The creature crawled out of the ravine, looked at Neilalive in front of it. Neilalive instructed telepathically, "I was waiting for you. Now go do what you are meant to do and wreak havoc."

Chapter-12

Hounds And Hallucinations

It was a good idea to have a club "***the Deciphers club,***"and House of nothing appeared to be the best location for operations. My benevolent friend Michael was all ready to take the charge of heading the club and planned the investigative activities. What if we sound esoteric. It was quite obvious that we would have to wrestle initially in order to navigate paradoxes. To our surprise we didn't have to wait longer.

Although meeting Mr. Golfer Décor, was no less than a feeling of perilously close to, when he mentioned that he too has encountered the hound.

Mr. Golfer described the hound as a six-feet-high black-eyed beast with sharp teeth and thick white claws.

I could recall the journal 'the devil's heart' displayed a creature fitting to the description "**Waho.**" It takes the form of your fear, and rest was unknown. We were confident and clear that this was not a hoax.

Mystery explorers were supposed to have an altogether a different ability, who dare to reach beyond and ultimately acquire superpowers.

I was sure this case would lead me to Neilalive again.

Date???

Location: shadow sea

Michael: Was it too late to help him? Would he be fine ....

Tannie: I hope that others were not hurt. We got separated coming here.

Michael: Did you hear those sounds like we had been followed?

(Distorted noises in the background)

Chapter-13

Man In The Grey Coat

I could feel a pang of guilt creeping up inside me. I had been keeping within me. On the one hand I was confident that my friends would understand me and be fascinated and thrilled to know about journals, strange perilous encounters with deadly mystical creatures, Other secrets and mysteries awaiting to be solved. On the other hand, I couldn't shake the feelings of apprehension and unwanted consequences that was still gnawing at me. What if they didn't believe me, What if they thought I was crazy, what if I lost their friendship because of this. It may really prove to be a risky affair as I may lose them forever as team.

As we gathered this morning at the House of nothing. I could feel the anxiety building up inside me. I had been keeping. I started right from meeting the masked man. As I continued I could see the excitement building in their eyes. They seemed to be amazed and very excited to know how they were part of the adventure. As the conversation wound down, I told my friends how sorry I was for not sharing this with them sooner. To my surprise they were understanding. They were completely enthralled to see Picheals.

The next day

Tannie was managing calls, Julia was trying to get well versed with the journals, and Michael was engaged in planning.

Michael and I were engrossed in listening to the narrative of an ambiguous situation occurred recently with Mr. Frank while he was on an adventure to a wild cavern near simpleton street in 'Tejangolan'

He narrated, "Like most of the people I too was not a believer that there exists a shadow world until I experienced on my own. It was a dusk but still enough light to see inside the cavern. I froze and looked ahead on the trail. A black form, a man in grey coat. As I stared, looked closer It stood about 6-7 feet tall, it resembled my father, who died three years ago. The very next moment the darkness in this thing appeared to resemble smoke. It had a rolling, billowing appearance. It crouched in a squatting position, stood up and vanished. It was the freakiest thing I've ever seen. I stood there for several seconds just looking wide eyes. I took a step forward and heard the sprinting sound, Leaves and sticks snapping under the weight of something but could see nothing! I double timed it back to the street. To this day I have only told a few people with similar experiences and I still have no idea who was the man in grey coat. It really shook my beliefs and I've been looking for answers ever since.

My friends and I had no comments on Mr. Frank's mystical experience. But we were sure of treading there the next day. The place was full of giant rocks, the wild caverns.

All that was required as if it were a creature described in the journals, how we recognize it and save ourselves.

It was mentioned in the fourth journal that the unique smelling seeds of Minsoi flower can attract the creature. I learnt by heart the different mystic spells, (given in the fourth journal) by which creature could be overpowered. We collected the seeds of Minsoi as many as we could.

10:45 pm

I felt very clear by purpose what for and where were we heading to , but at the same time was feeling very vulnerable. My mind was racing all the time. I was going to accomplish so much.

Tannie and I felt that we are at our best when together. Sometimes, disruptions in the thought process occur and senses get magnified. Owing it all to some extra dopamine, serotonin, and noradrenaline in my synapses, that was making me reach new dimensions. I was exploring different realities. Unravelling a whole new world in front of me was no more my imagination but an experience and reality. Michael and Julia have moved into the next cavern.

We waited for the creature to make his move after spreading the seeds of Minsoi. Soon to our dismay, The man in the grey coat, who was moving was caught by my peripheral vision. It was definitely not an illusion or my mind playing tricks on me. It was moving very fast and changing shapes of distorted images of human shape smoke. All the weird visuals might be the strange way to interact through these split second visions giving the feeling of some sort of higher dimension. We were following desperately it was changing its forms. It was none other than Waho. It is Him we were after and he successfully managed to hide from us.

The Waho was trying to escape. I hurriedly enchanted a spell that was strong enough to trap him.

(*As Ryan Anderson enchants a spell The skies light up. Ryan Anderson enchants another spell and pulls it in a rock*). Finally, it was defeated. I trapped Waho's energy in a rock using the Alchemy grimoire. I hid the rock into the forest and marked the place.

Later that night

I am back to my room but my mind was on a fast-forwarding mode about the cavern incident happened yesterday. I have been seeing them constantly with my mind's eye. On the other hand, the paranoia, an eerie feeling that somebody you can't see is watching you. Such ripples in our realm may drive anyone crazy. But I believed in guardians guiding me through journals

Chapter-14

Anger And The Heat

I was reading through the 'Alchemy grimoire'. There were artifacts that secret societies used since the founding era to protect people from unseen horrors. Strange enough, only a little was described about this foundation era.

The house shown in the journal belonged to Miss Channel, who lived with her kids in the neighborhood. Michael mentioned his dad was once a good friend of the Miss Channel. Off late people were talking about surreal experiences whenever they visited her place. People started calling her perpetrator.

When we entered her building, it was empty, Miss Channel seemed as if she is either under hypnosis or some debilitating fear. She was acting strange and not responding to anything. Not even acknowledging our presence. We were all in a state of cringe. In the very next moment with a sudden flash of light, someone appeared behind Michael. It looked like Arman, but it was not him because he looked a little different as if it was his doppelganger. He grabbed Tannie's arm with his talons. I moved towards Tannie to help her, a flash of lightning was all around us. He disappeared. Though it would sound crazy, there was a lightening man. I woke up from trance and realized that I had regressed to my childhood. But who actually was the hypnotist. Miss Channel ? It was a strange sensation indeed.

We all four met at the House of nothing. Michael Tannie and Julia also shared the similar experience of hypnosis. We felt really challenged on our memory retrieval. No body remembered what actually happened at Miss channels place.

The doors started to move so were the windows fluttering like leaves; a tall guy comes out of the house in a ragged clothes blonde hair and patchy skin with a tint of blue in his eyes, walking up to me. I was getting the intuition to be ready for the next jarring encounter.

'I am the Zealot of Curse Cunner'" as he introduced himself. I could see its glinted eyes blazing with dark power.

He asked me to follow him to the Curse Cunner for some exchanges. I was in fear and defiance. Despite knowing I cannot trifled with, still I was trying to weigh my options.

"Fine'," I said at last, in a resigned voice "Lead the way." The zealot smirked triumphantly, then turned and began to lead the way through the forest. I was alert for any signs of danger.

The zealot was suddenly attacked by none other than Neilalive. After a barrage of powerful attacks one bright flash from the sky pulled zealot inside the Neilalive, and every single atom in his body was obliterated.

After a few minutes, a similar-looking creature bows down to Neilalive as if he had remade the zealot to his choosing.

The Alchemy grimoire started vibrating and glowing violently. Devils Heart was flipping pages.

At home the candle fell from the shelf on the journal codex and got illuminated on its own.

The next thing I knew, I once again got back to my senses from another shot of hypnosis. I saw in the mirror the strange image. Who was the cursed cunner, and how is he related to Neilalive?

Some hours later

I reached Michael's house, it was crazy to know that he too had similar clip. We both had same idea about the cursed cunner that he was on our side, and was under threat of Neilalive. Later in the day when we met Tannie and Julia, finding the similar episode now was quite expected.

We connected the dots trying to figure out if the person was real. We reached House of nothing to set out to explore the abandoned mansion completely.

We sensed foreboding as we made our way through the dusty, cobwebbed rooms. Our foot steps echoing through the empty halls. As we descended into the basement, we could feel the temperature drop with air growing thick, we found a pit, a gaping hole in the ground seemed to lead nowhere, we were shuddered at the thought of what could be down there? Tannie, Julia and Michael quickly made their way back onto the attic. I stayed back or rather I would say I was made to stay back. Suddenly a chill ran down my spine as I saw a figure materialize out of nowhere. It was dark, shadowy figure, hovering in the air. It was me, Ryan Anderson, I rubbed my eyes as it seemed moving closer. I tried to scream but no sound would come out of my throat. The whispering gradually grew louder as if thousand voices all speaking at once. Shrouded with fear, I could feel my heart pounding in my chest. Finally, with a bust of courage I confronted," Who are you?" with my shaking voice, my voice was barely above a whisper. It's eyes glowed with other worldly light and it replied, "I am a being of the void and I can veil your reality". "I have come to show you the glimpse of what lies beyond". Your future is entangled in your past, but you have no history, so where did you come from?

The words echoed in my mind. I could sense a powerful energy emanating from it. This was too surreal, something uncanny and almost hypnotic about it. My vision began to blur. When my eyes cleared I found myself at the attic with my friends. The attic was massive with towering ceilings and large windows that looked out over the town. But as I gazed out at the view with awe and wonder, I was feeling with strange compulsion to share this unique incident with my friends but ultimately decided to keep it to me only.

(As Ryan and his friends were checking out the House of nothing from the basement to the attic. something was going on in the dark forest, home of the deadliest creatures. It was between Curse cunner and Neilalive. These two powerful evil forces were constantly at odds with each other. Was it after the five mystical journals?

Chapter-15

Here Comes Trouble

The "devil's heart" and the "Alchemy grimoire" started glowing all of a sudden as if I was in danger, but as soon as I opened them, they stopped shining.

I heard the sound of something had with thud. As I opened the door to see. The masked man was lying on the ground.

"NEILALIVE, don't spare him Ryan, your life is in danger too". Screamed Arman Before he fell unconscious. I couldn't bear to see him in such a deteriorated condition. Neilalive will have to pay for what it had done. Fueled by my anger and my desire to revenge and protect those around me from the dangers of the mystical world, no matter what come may, I have to be ready for whatever challenges lay ahead.

Facing Neilalive was the only option I had. How am I supposed to fight something 'shrouded in mystery'?

I knew how Neilalive had made its appearance evident.

The wind interacted with the topography to create a powerful barely audible hum to a sharp beam of high-pitched noise as if hundreds of marbles rolling along the ground. This induced a terrible headache, dizziness, panic, dread, chills, nervousness, raised heartbeat rate, and difficulty in breathing eventually leading to concussions. That's was precisely how Neilalive effected with its appearance

I spent the next few days training myself tirelessly, honing my combat skills and preparing for the inevitable confrontation.

I was armed with a sound proof spell that kept me sentient. I continued to the woods all alone. The trees started to shake violently as a dense fog came around me, and there he was right in front of me. It emerged from the shadows, It's eyes glowing with malevolent energy. Neilalive looked at me with those eyes as his strange tentacles-like parts moved in the sky.

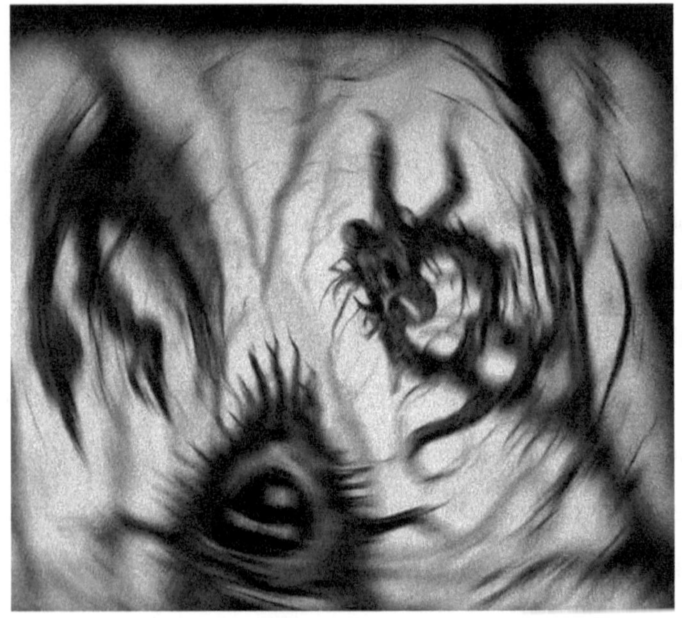

"Here I am, Ryan Anderson. Were you looking for me ? "His spooky loud voice was clearly audible. It had special ability to communicate in the language human can understand. I could feel the power coursing through me. I garnered enough courage to face the unfathomed apparition. We clashed in a fierce battle, exchanging blows and spells.

My body was once again paralyzed with fear seeing the terrifying thing in the town now in front of me and what he said next was chilling to the bones.

Neilalive said, "You think you are the one I am hunting? No, my dear boy, it is what you will become. That's what I am after. You are nothing, not even an ounce of what you will become. I will find you when the time comes, you'll be bestowed with a fate worse than eternal torture". Then Neil alive moved around, me laughing and then disappeared into the fog.

Chapter-16

Fighting For What

It had been almost a week, The fear had sunken deep and remained in the dark forest, allowance, and helplessness.

I couldn't gather any strength to speak or do anything. Tannie came up with a suggestion I should meet the Professor Nomed who was a renowned, naturalist and known for studying creatures in the world. He spent his entire life traveling to remote corners of the earth. The town people were wary of the professor rumored that he was a dark force, quite enigmatic and mysterious figure. People believed that he was connected to the paranormal world. He was known for his eccentric behavior. Professor's house was surrounded by rare herbs and plants and he had many creatures' specimens in his laboratory with whom he could almost communicate. He had vast knowledge about deadly creatures.

I agreed to approach the professor cautiously unsure of what to make of him.

“Hello, Ryan, Welcome” The Professor said smiling at me. It’s good to finally meet you”. He greeted me and let me inside the house. I was taken aback but tried hard to keep my composure.

He spoke with a deep gravelly voice and his eyes glowed with an otherworldly light.

I apologize if I startled you. I have a of sensing things about people. Its part of what makes me good at my job.

I nodded, still feeling a bit unnerved

I had an intuition that he did have some super natural powers. I tried to act cool and told him about the aura he has. He pretended to be the guardian of the natural world. His true intentions were hard to discern.

I felt a jolt of surprise and apprehension when he indirectly mentioned while speaking that he is looking for five secret journals for his research which I may know about.

I'm sorry, I don't know what you're talking about," I stammered, trying to play dumb also trying to make my voice steady.

The professor seemed to sensed my hesitation. He continued, with gentle tone.

"If you're willing to share your journals I can help you with insights that would glean from the secret journals". He said firmly while looking skeptically at me.

I wasn't sure whether I could trust him. Still couldn't help but feel a sense of unease. I shifted uncomfortably in my seat wondering if I should make a run for it.

He took a deep breath, looked into his piercing gaze at me and said," Ryan you are in a process of healing I am aware of what all you had gone through. You need to understand the exhilarating power of journals to uncover the mysteries that I can only help you with".

There was a feeling of sudden sense of ominous and danger as if I am being trapped.

As the professor continued to speak, I felt a sudden surge of determination. I couldn't let him control me. I feigned in what professor was saying, nodded along as he spoke. Despite my reservations I continued to listen. Meanwhile my mind raced trying to overcome his persuasiveness.

I finally mustered the courage to leave the house with the agreement to give him the journals soon. I walked away from his house and felt a sense of closure but also intrigued. I was back to my own self of being ever ready to face Neilalive again head-on, armed with my own intuition and commitment to my cause.

Chapter-17

When Will This End?

Neilalive is still at large, and I am lost for words.

Meanwhile dark cave a few miles away

It will be our secret, and it will kill him.

Laughter fades in the background as something ominous is about to occur, changing the fate of the entire Tejangolan.

I have seen people act strangely here; is everything an act? The thought terrifies me to the core. I saw a family happy but the moment. I walked away. They just stood there silently, smiling.

My journals are the only clue to solving these puzzles.

As you all know, I called my first journal the codex, which is written in a strange language.

The second journal (devil's' heart) was written about mysteries for guidance, and the third book (white void) has empty thick pages with an unusual texture.

The fourth book was about the lost art of Alchemy; I will be honest; it was not what I imagined; Alchemy here was different from any that I had ever heard.

It was about the knowledge on how to unlock the connection between our world and another of overlapping universe. Every spell and incantation.

Every spell in the grimoire has a counter spell, it seemed that the journal was warning about the dangers of wielding too much power.

The fifth journal was still a mystery to me. It was not meant to be opened and its secrets could not be wielded by mere mortals. It seemed almost indestructible with incredible power. Unlocking its secrets could have dire consequences.

One odd day , Julia and I walked through the woods, the blowing wind made trees to bend as if they were bowing to a king.

, the devil's heart started glowing again, and I stopped and opened it mentioned something called

The Fike

Power becomes anything you desire

Source- constant thoughts regarding the desires

Shape, size

Color and physical body unknown.

The way to defeat is to lose your desires and let it all go.

I did not understand what the journal was trying to tell me, so I stood at the spot to figure out what it meant, but no luck thus far. I decided to keep moving forward. I started to give up my curiosity, I began to sense a subtle ringing sensation in the ear!

It turned out that the only thing stopping me from fearing and moving to a new place was my curiosity, I had lost it, I felt strange as if I am possessed, a part of me had gone forever. Julia was the sole witness to what all had happened. All I remembered was Julia kept on with her soothing words, “Ryan, it will be all okay, believe in yourself because all of us do believe in you with all our hearts”. It takes courage to go head-on with this kind of world, and we are fortunate to have you help us through it”. She said. All I knew at that moment that I would never lose one thing. This new friendship.

The sky was red as blood after the sunset.

A dark fog engulfed the forest, Silence was in the air as Ryan walked back home with Julia through the forest in the evening.

Chapter–18

Biggest Mysteries Of The Town Yet?

31 January 2023

Everything going around me was connected in some way. All I had to do was figure it out; the journals were the key, and my friends were the hands. The lock was the mystery around; those creatures were not ghosts. They were far more dangerous because they were real!

(Throughout centuries there had been paranormal stories, but in Tejangolan, nothing is just a story, it is as real as it gets).

5 February 2023

I was going through the Professor's lab behind his house when I saw a plant and a few symbols; they looked familiar, as if I had seen them somewhere, but I couldn't recall.

The streets had been tranquil, with no new cases and nothing new going on at school.

I kept on having nightmares as if I'm stuck in a vast prison; all I could see was blurry light coming from a hole.

My intrusive thoughts still made me feel restless as if I was missing something. Was that something right in front of me? Could that be dreams? Or Something mysterious about the Neilalive, waiting to get unraveled. Which might just flip the board entirely. The prison I saw in my dreams was the prison I have to break in order unfold the sealed destiny. What was really missing? I was stuck like quicksand. The more I was trying to find a way out, the deeper was I sinking.

I tried to open the "locked destiny" several times but didn't get any far, just a clue that the journal will open when the prison will break.

10 February 2023

Something had changed. As if there had been a colossal incident, the leaves of the trees around the town had continuously been moving, made a rustling sound. Though there was no wind blowing. The air around was absolutely still. The streets of Tejangolan were empty. There were sudden tremors in the ground, and the "devil's heart" stopped responding.

Bhaskara enters the town, walks across the House of nothing to the doorstep of Ryan Anderson, and rings the bell...

Are you willing to keep going further to uncover the truth in the strange world of Ryan Anderson?

Where mystery thrives at every corner? There is more to come, and Ryan's journey has just begun.

The path needs to be straight. Time is running out. Ryan must follow his instincts and be careful whom to ally himself with because in Tejangolan.

TRUST NO ONE

To be continued…

9 789357 040358

Printed by Libri Plureos GmbH in Hamburg,
Germany